Just So Long As You're Happy

AMY LAURENS

OTHER WORKS

SANCTUARY SERIES

Where Shadows Rise
Through Roads Between
When Worlds Collide

KADITEOS SERIES

How Not To Acquire A Castle

STORM FOXES SERIES

A Fox of Storms and Starlight

SHORTER WORKS

Bones Of The Sea
Darkness And Good
Dreaming Of Forests
It All Changes Now
Rush Job
Trust Issues

NON-FICTION

How To Write Dogs
How To Theme
How To Create Cultures
How To Create Life
How To Map
The 32 Worst Mistakes People Make About Dogs

Find other works by the author at
www.amylaurens.com

Just So Long As You're Happy

INKLET #63

AMY LAURENS

Inkprint PRESS

www.inkprintpress.com

Print ISBN: 978-1-925825-65-7
eBook ISBN: 9798201914226

www.inkprintpress.com

National Library of Australia Cataloguing-in-Publication Data
Laurens, Amy 1985 –
Just So Long As You're Happy
44 p.
ISBN: 978-1-925825-65-7
Inkprint Press, Canberra, Australia
1. Fiction—Fantasy—Contemporary. 2. Fiction—Short Stories

First Print Edition: August 2021
Cover photo © Enrique Meseguer via Pixabay
Cover design © Inkprint Press
Interior art © Amy Laurens

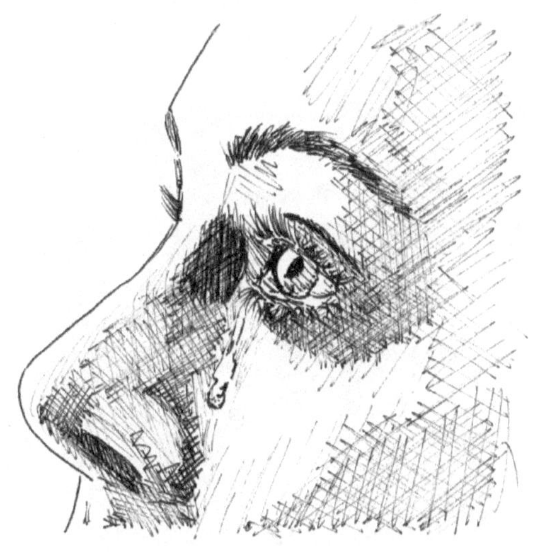

JUST SO LONG AS YOU'RE HAPPY

IT WOULD BE EASY TO WRITE THIS STORY flippantly, because Morgan was a flippant kind of girl—or at least, that was what everybody told her. She was flippant, they said, because she never took anything seriously, always got what she wanted, never told anybody how she really felt. She had dark glossy locks and perfect brown eyes, Junior Gaultier dresses and Alexander Mc-Queen shoes—and a memory with crystal clarity of the time she'd overheard her mother whispering in the bedroom to the man Morgan had called Daddy: *She's not yours. It's all my fault. How can you forgive me?*

Morgan couldn't, but Mummy had not been talking to her, so Morgan did what everybody told her to: she became flippant.

And the fact that the man called Daddy never really met her eye, never offered hugs or kisses, always turned his face away when tucking her in at night... That was okay, because Morgan could make him love her anyway. Morgan could make anyone love her.

Of course, she didn't realise how truly special that was until she was in school; until then she'd—reasonably—assumed that all little girls were adored by everyone, that anyone could make other people feel special just by smiling at them, that the natural proclivity of the world to follow her orders was just nature taking form.

But then, when she was eight, Morgan found Amber crying behind the shed at school.

"They're bullying me," Amber had mumbled through tear-streaked lips. "They hate me."

Morgan rocked back on her heels. "So make them like you!"

Amber shook her head. "I don't know how! It's easy for you. Everyone loves you. All you have to do is, is, exist!" Amber's eyes grew narrow as she flung herself to her feet. "Well, I don't love you. I hate you! I hate you and your stupid hair and your stupid smile, and everybody else is just stupid!"

Morgan did what she always did when confronted with conflict, and shot Amber a beaming smile.

"Don't!" Amber shouted, stomping her foot and fisting her hands. "Don't do that to me! If I don't want to like you, then I don't have to!" And off she stormed.

Morgan leaned back against the shed and frowned. All she'd done was smile. But then again, she'd expected it to work, and it hadn't. Maybe Amber was right. Maybe Morgan *was* making people like her, only not in an ordinary way.

Morgan ran her lip between her teeth until she tasted blood. If she could make people like her, then Daddy… She chomped down hard on her lip and rose to her feet.

No. It didn't matter. It didn't matter why he loved her, only that he did.

And that was how it was—until Christmas. About a week before the Big Day, which in Morgan's designer-filled world absolutely deserved capitalisation, she overheard a second conversation that made her freeze on the spot: as she wandered nonchalantly past her parents' room, not at all trying to scout out hints of upcoming gifts, she heard her father.

"Chloe, no," he said. "I'm not buying her anything. You've got to stop indulging her like this. She's going to figure it out one day, if she hasn't already, and…" He trailed off, and Morgan realised it was because her mother had begun to cry.

I can fix this, she thought blankly. *My mother is crying, and I can fix it.*

And as she stood with her palm pressed against the cold, smooth paint of the bedroom door, that was what she focused on: not the fact that Daddy, who in point of fact was probably only Daddy because Morgan blistered him with radiant smiles day and night, had figured out her trick; not the fact that he was planning to punish her by withholding Christmas presents; not the fact that he was trying to turn her mother against her and make Mummy hate her too.

Just the fact that Mummy was crying, and she could make it stop.

Morgan pushed open the door.

Daddy glared at her over Mummy's shoulder. "Morgan, this isn't—"

Morgan held up one hand, only dimly aware of the tears that spilled over the edges of her eyelashes, like the one extra drop a teaspoon couldn't quite contain.

Somewhere, in some world, Morgan was crying, and she knew it; but here and now, Mummy was crying, and that was all that mattered.

Morgan stared at Daddy until his glare melted and stared into nothing. Instead, he rocked Mummy back and forth mechanically, patting her as steadily as a metronome.

Morgan walked closer and touched Mummy's leg.

Mummy jumped, twisting around in Daddy's arms so that his pats fell awkwardly on her chest.

She tried to brush him away, but he swayed and patted, swayed and patted, locked into motion at Morgan's command.

Dimly, Morgan thought that maybe she could feel guilty for that. But he wasn't Daddy anyway, was he, and he only loved her because she used her smile on him.

"Morgan, sweetie, what's wrong?" Mummy said, scrubbing the tears from her own eyes.

Morgan gazed at her, eyes on a level as Mummy sat on the edge of her bed. "Don't be sad," Morgan whispered.

Mummy gave a half smile. "Oh sweetheart." She reached for Morgan.

Morgan drew in a deep breath and resisted. "No. Mummy." She paused to make sure she had Mummy's full attention. "Don't be sad."

This time, she felt it as it happened, much more clearly than she'd ever felt it before—and she'd been looking for it ever since Amber had declared that she hated her.

Something went out of Morgan as she spoke, swirling in the air for a moment before coming to rest in her mother's eyes—and Mummy, who'd been opening her mouth to speak, instead settled back into Daddy's embrace with her eyes dancing and her lips quirking up in a smile.

"Morgan!" she said delightedly. "What do you want, darling?"

Morgan, tears no longer flowing, head aching from the screams she felt inside, searched her mother's smiling face and nodded. "Nothing, Mummy," she said. "As long as you're happy."

"Oh, Darling!" Her mother's smile stretched. "I've never been so happy in all my life."

This time, when Mummy reached out, Morgan let herself be drawn into a hug, and together the three of them rocked as Daddy swayed and patted

like a metronome, and Mummy hum-
med like the happiest bee in the world.

THE MAKING OF *JUST SO LONG AS YOU'RE HAPPY*

This was an exploratory backstory kind of story. Morgan is the protagonist of a probable-trilogy of young adult contemporary fantasy novels, and she is hilarious. However, as you can see from this story, she comes with a dark past: if you can manipulate other people's emotions (sometimes without realising it), how can you ever actually be sure that people love you?

Poor Morgan.

One day I'll figure out how the arc of her novels is supposed to go and write that whole story; she is actually a hilariously voicey protagonist as a teenager, and is super fun to write!

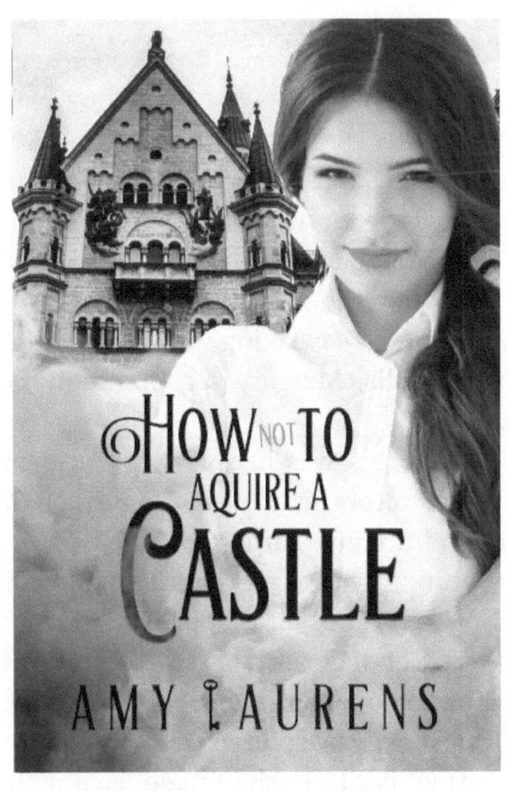

HOW NOT TO ACQUIRE A CASTLE

CHAPTER ONE

ON A HARD PLASTIC CHAIR IN THE FRONT row of the Great Hall in the world's fifth-best evil overlording academy, with its red-wooden parquetry floor that spoke of wealth and the beige, square panels of sound-boards speaking of conservatism on the walls, Mercury sat, pointedly not sweating.

Partly, this was because the Academy Administrators had deigned to turn on the air-conditioning earlier in the day, in recognition of the fact that the hall would be packed out with approximately six hundred bodies, all here to celebrate the graduation of about a third of that crowd.

But mostly, Mercury was pointedly not sweating because she made it a point never to sweat, sweat being an indication that she was working hard, and hard work being antithetical to her way of life.

However. If she *had* been sweating right now, it would not have been due to the uncomfortable warmth of six hundred packed bodies that even the air-conditioning system couldn't completely shift, or, in fact, from overexertion. Instead, it would have been caused by an even more unfamiliar concept in Mercury's emotional vocabulary: nervousness.

Mercury did not *get* nervous. Mercury got things *done*.

So the fact that she was sitting here, in the front row of the Great Hall, about to graduate from Evil Overlording Academy (with distinction), and was feeling *nervous*... She crumpled the black paper program in her pale fists. It made her furious, that's what it did.

Abjectly furious, that snooty-tooty Deviran with his stupid morals and his stupid I-don't-want-to-be-here and his stupid Overlords-are-empty-figureheads and his stupid face sitting ten people over, looking implacable with his deep brown skin and barely-there, precision-groomed beard, as though he knew it gave him a stupid air of alluringly stupid mystery…

Mercury scowled and searched for the train of thought that had been derailed, yet again, by Deviran's stupidity.

Ah. Yes. She was angry because she was nervous because she wasn't absolutely entirely one hundred and fifty percent sure that she'd beaten Deviran in their final exams, and 1) being anything less than a hundred and fifty percent certain of anything made her cranky, and 2) being beaten by Deviran for dux of the year would be utterly unbearable. She flicked away a piece of fluff that had become snagged under her immaculately magenta-painted nails and smoothed out the black paper program.

In the front corner of the hall, the starkly-attired string quartet with their traditional black instruments began playing the March of the Oncoming Doom. The screechy scrapes of hundreds of chairs on the hall's wooden floor sounded as the crowd climbed to its collective feet.

Mercury sat with her arms firmly folded for a few moments longer, until her best friend Sparky kicked her in the ankle.

"Get up, idiot," Sparky hissed, hints of real flame flickering through her flame-coloured pixie cut.

"No," Mercury said, flouncing to her feet and tossing her own glossy brown hair back over her shoulders. Four years she'd been playing by the Academy's rules in order to get what she wanted, and she'd had just about enough. Other people's rules should only be applied to plebs too stupid to invent their own.

Sparky rolled her eyes somewhere over Mercury's head before focusing on the stage, where the ceremonial party had begun entering.

Mercury clenched her jaw and narrowed her own eyes as the teachers of the Evil Overlording Academy filed onto the stage, dressed in their formal finery. Each teacher had their own distinctive look that matched their personality and their Overlording style, from severe charcoal suits to jet-black leathers, pastel ball-gowns and gem-toned lingerie and eye-blinding spandex, and even on one tiny old woman at the back, worn jeans and a grey flannel shirt. She was the one to watch out for, of course; Mercury could respect an Overlord who was confident enough in their abilities that they didn't need to telegraph them. It wasn't a look *she* would consider, of course, but still. She could respect it.

The band's march finished and, after a moderately awkward pause, the crowd sat. The Principal, pale skin and dark hair matching his suspiciously vampiric red-and-black suit, took the podium, and Mercury narrowed her eyes. He was doing a superb job of hiding his emotions—he was a premier Evil Overlord, after all—but she was Mercury, and unlike anyone else, she had the benefit of being able to rummage through people's consciousnesses. She was better at adding things *into* people's minds than taking information out, but he was telegraphing fear loudly enough that she could sense it without trying overly much.

Mercury pursed her lips.

Hmm.

The Principal cleared his throat at the blackened-wood podium, and the fear made it into his usually-unreadable eyes. "Before we begin," he said, and Mercury's stomach did a peculiar kind of flip-flop. "I have a pressing announcement to make regarding the safety of our students and their families."

He cleared his throat again and took out a sheet of paper from his pocket, unfolding it carefully and smoothing out the creases before beginning again. "The Council"—quiet booing echoed around the hall, and Mercury tsked impatiently—"have asked me to recommend that students from Tumul Tuos seriously consider postponing their return to town for a few days. The city is dealing with a *situation* at present which may present a danger to our students' health and safety."

Mercury's hands fisted at her sides and she forced herself to remain seated. What was wrong with her city? What had the Council mucked up now? A risk to the students' safety? There had to be more he wasn't telling them. Gently, Mercury tugged on his consciousness, implanting the suggestion that it might be better to share the news than to keep it secret. After all, how could they fight an enemy they didn't know?

"There are, ah..." He trailed off, glancing side to side as though wondering why his mouth had decided to continue.

Mercury didn't snicker, but she did press her lips together in satisfaction.

The Principal took a deep, steadying breath and seemed to change tack. "There has been one death already. The family have already been notified, so it is with much regret that I must inform you that Woovermyer will no longer be with us at the Evil Overlording Academy."

Murmurs broke out around the room, not all of them sad—to be expected in a school devoted to raising the next generation of dictators (ish) and despots (of sorts).

Mercury, however, crushed her program in her left hand, fist so tight her nails bit her palm.

"You okay?" Sparky murmured.

Mercury gave a single, tense shake of her head and stared at the podium. Dead. Livie Woovermyer was dead in *her city*. And the Council hadn't done anything to stop it. Couldn't do anything to stop it, probably, given they'd warned the students to stay away. Livie hadn't been the strongest candidate in the year level, but she was no lightweight, either. It would take a lot of power to kill a Seven.

Enough was enough. A good thing Mercury was about to graduate at the top of the class, giving her the right to knock the lowest ranking current Overlord off their perch. Tumul Tuos would be hers in a matter of hours. And then there'd be no more of these wasteful deaths. Her city would be safe at last.

Madame Pompadour was up the front now, elbow gloves the same glimmery silver colour as her elaborate, piled-curls wig, eyelids gleaming with matching silver eye shadow, and abruptly Mercury realised Madame was there to make the announcement that would change her life forever. She leaned forward in her seat, ready to stand when her name was called.

"And now the announcement you've all been dying for," the Political Alliances teacher trilled, the frills on her evening gown fluttering as she moved. "The dux of this year's cohort!"

Sweat slicked Mercury's palms. Irritated, she reached over and wiped them on Sparky's thigh.

Sparky pushed Mercury's hands back into her own personal space bubble and Mercury, nervous to the edge of distraction, let her.

"Will you please join me in welcoming to the stage, our wonderful dux for this year, Deviran Goodsmith!"

Mercury froze halfway to standing. "Did she just say Deviran?" she whispered furiously to Sparky.

Sparky hauled her forcibly back down into her seat. "Yes," she hissed back. "Sit down, you're making a fool of yourself."

Mercury's spine snapped upright as she sat, and she arranged the folds of her long black skirt demurely. "No I'm not." She closed her eyes. "Deviran's going up to the stage, isn't he?" Even at a whisper, the misery in her voice was clear, but this time, she didn't care.

Sparky reached over and squeezed her hand.

Mercury squeezed back, lacing her fingers through Sparky's, and held tight as all her plans and dreams vanished in front of her.

A stone had landed in her chest. That must be it. Some strange sort of magic that made her chest contract and sink, and made the world distort for just a moment, long enough to trick her into thinking Deviran had beaten her so that someone could jump in front of her and yell SURPRISE!

Any moment now.

Any moment.

She refused to open her eyes and watch Deviran parading across the stupid stage like some stupid stupid-person, receiving his stupid medal and stupid symbolic crest pin.

It was that last exam question.

She'd known Deviran would pull out his ridiculous 'Evil Overlords are merely figureheads, the Business Guild is where the power really lies' rant that everyone had heard a million times back when he was younger and angrier, and she'd tried to counter it, she really had.

She'd argued for the importance of the Overlording position, for the power of having a symbolic figure to unite the population in their hatred, for having a person able to make all the difficult, necessary decisions the Council was too weak and spineless to make... But it hadn't been enough. Everything she'd worked for, everything she'd set out to prove—and it wasn't enough.

There were words, there were names, and then forever later, once she'd died twice already, Sparky elbowed her in the ribs. "Come on," Sparky muttered. "We're up next."

And sure enough, there was a shuffling of presenters as the last of the Powers Behind The Thone graduates departed the stage, and the next speaker announced in

threatening, funereal tones, "The Overlording cohort."

Mercury blinked furiously and followed
Sparky to the end of the line at the right
side of the stage. The other candidates
proceeded one at a time across the stage,
two girls and then stupid Deviran, and
then a handful more and then Sparky, and
then the speaker was calling her name.

Hands fisted, Mercury tossed her head
high, climbed the four steps, and marched
across the stage. She wouldn't look at
them, the stupid faculty who'd denied her
the city she rightfully deserved, and she
wouldn't look the other way either, at the
classmates and crowd undoubtedly snig-
gering at her failure.

She shook hands with the presenter,
and while he pinned the tiny crossed-
swords badge on her collar, her eyes
betrayed her and slid towards the aud-
ience. Her stomach flipped as she saw the
crowd of parents and friends behind the
rows of students, all the way to the back
of the hall, twenty rows at least, illum-
inated by the late afternoon light stream-

ing in through the ceiling-high windows to the right. Everyone had someone here to watch them graduate. Everyone except Weird Al—and her.

The presenter finished with her pin, muttered something to her, and offered his hand again. Mercury coldly ignored it and strode from the stage. It didn't matter. None of it mattered. Tumul Tuos was her city anyway, and no one could change that. She'd think of something. She'd take a day or two out, make some plans…

And she could always hope that Deviran would choose some other Overlording territory. He'd be stupid to, but then again, he was stupid, so. Mercury could hope.

All at once, mid-way down the steps off the stage, Mercury came to rigid attention, scanning the room. Somewhere out there in the crowd, an exchange of power had just taken place, and it felt… unusual.

But the final few students were backing up behind her and muttering, so Mercury headed back toward her seat, craning her head all the while and searching for some sign of whatever it was that had just discharged a dizzyingly quiet amount of power into the room.

She sat, and Sparky leaned over. "Okay?"

"Mm," said Mercury. "Did you feel…" She accidentally caught the eye of the student behind her and twisted back to face the front.

"Feel what?"

Mercury turned it over in her mind. It had felt like a large shot of power discharged very quietly—but perhaps it hadn't been. Perhaps it had only been a small discharge after all, something most people wouldn't have noticed.

But still, something about it had tugged on her. It very nearly felt like something she'd felt before, only she *knew* she'd never sensed that kind of discharge before.

She shook her head. "Never mind. Don't worry."

Sparky sighed and straightened. "It's fine, Mercury," she said, drily exasperated.

"I know you didn't win, but I promise, you'll live through it."

Mercury waved a hand for silence.

The power had just discharged again, and it had come from somewhere in the back corner, far away from the windows and light.

Impatiently, Mercury waited for the formalities to conclude. The crowd stood while the quartet played the exit march, and the stage party left, Mercury tapping her foot all the while.

The moment the last notes of the march died away, Mercury turned and headed to the back corner, weaving in and out of the students and parents who had seemed to explode slowly but inexorably out from the neat rows of seating, ignoring Sparky's calls behind her. Power, something that tugged in a way that was strange and familiar, all at once. She pushed her way through a family posing for pictures—and halted.

In the shadows of the back corner, Deviran stood with his family, with his stupid, smug little smile, looking as tall and dark and stupidly alluring as ever. Prat.

His mother, short but sleek, and his father—tall, and utterly terrifying in a way not at all diminished by his gleaming smile—gushed over him, patting his back and hugging him tight. Within moments the Principal was there, glibly shaking hands and congratulating them on the success of their son. Something flickered across his consciousness, and also Deviran's father's—some moment of recognition in response to what they were saying.

But Mercury brushed it aside just as the mother brushed melodramatic tears from her cheeks and handed Deviran a silver-wrapped package about as long as her hand but half the width.

That. That was the source of the strange, magical feeling. Mercury watched hawk-eyed as Deviran unwrapped the gift. A glimpse of gold set her pulse racing— What was it? What did it do? Could she steal it?—and then the paper fell away to the floor, and Deviran stood staring wordlessly at the object in his hands, and Mercury did too.

Wide-eyed, Deviran raised his gaze to his parents, and even from where she stood Mercury could hear the reverence in his voice as he thanked them.

But Mercury had eyes only for the object. No wonder she'd felt it discharge, and no wonder it had felt both strange and familiar. In Deviran's hands lay a glorious, sunshine-gold key, large and strong—and with a handle in the shape of a stylised fish, long, flowing fins curving to make the grip.

A Key. They'd given him a Key. And not just any Key, but *the* Key, *her* Key, the Artefact of Power belonging to *her* city.

A wordless noise of wanting rose in Mercury's throat. Who cared about being dux? She needed that Key.

Keep reading! Head to
www.amylaurens.com/books/kaditeos/castle
to buy your copy now!

ABOUT THE AUTHOR

AMY LAURENS is an Australian author of fantasy fiction for all ages. She isn't able to manipulate people's emotions just by speaking at them… but then again, she is a writer, so maybe she does manipulate people's emotions through words.

Amy has also written the award-winning portal-fantasy *Sanctuary* series about Edge, a 13-year-old girl forced to move to a small country town because of witness protection (the first book is *Where Shadows Rise*), the humorous fantasy *Kaditeos* series, following newly graduated Evil Overlord Mercury as she attempts to acquire a castle, the young adult series *Storm Foxes,* about love and magic and family in small town Australia, and a whole host of non-fiction.

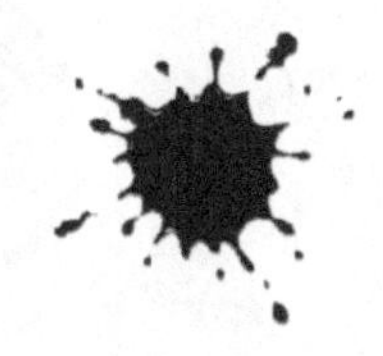

INKLETS

Collect them all! Released on the
1st and 15th of each month.

INKLET #055
Allure
AMY LAURENS

INKLET #056
The LIES We KNOW
LIANA BROOKS

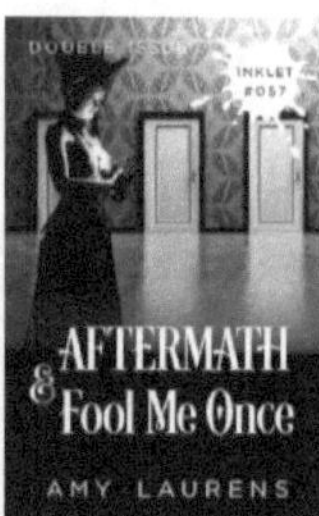

DOUBLE ISSUE
INKLET #057
AFTERMATH & Fool Me Once
AMY LAURENS

INKLET #058
Purity
An Age Of Unicorns Story
AMY LAURENS

INKLET #059
Saved
AMY LAURENS

INKLET #060
A Kiss is the Secret
AMY LAURENS

INKLET #061
A Changing Tides Story
Fire Bright
AMY LAURENS

INKLET #062
Hades AND Persephone
LIANA BROOKS

INKLET #063
Just So Long As You're Happy
AMY LAURENS

INKLET #064
Theft Of A Lifetime
LIANA BROOKS

INKLET #065
Shoe
AMY LAURENS

INKLET #066
Published AUTHOR
LIANA BROOKS

DOUBLE ISSUE
INKLET #067
THE REMARKABLE INSIGHT OF JELLYBEANS & Understanding
AMY LAURENS

INKLET #068
Desperate Measures
AMY LAURENS

INKLET #069
Rock-a-bye
LIANA BROOKS

INKLET #070
the Other Carly
AMY LAURENS

INKLET #071
By Bioluminescent Light
AMY LAURENS

INKLET #072
Even Villains Grant Wishes
A Heroes & Villains Story
LIANA BROOKS